EL DORADO COUNTY LIBRARY
3 1738 00432 3935

D0555838

ONCE UPON A BEDTIME STORY

ONCE UPON A BEDTIME STORY

Classic Tales Retold by JANE YOLEN
Illustrated by RUTH TIETJEN COUNCELL

Boyds Mills Press

To Maddison Jane, with love from Nana – J. Y.

To Eric, Aurora, and Daniel – R. T. C.

Published by Caroline House
Boyds Mills Press, Inc.
A Highlights Company
815 Church Street
Honesdale, Pennsylvania 18431
Printed in Hong Kong

Publisher Cataloging-in-Publication Data
Yolen, Jane.
Once upon a bedtime story : classic tales / retold by Jane Yolen ;
illustrated by Ruth Tietjen Councell.—1st ed.
[96]p. : col. ill. ; cm.
Summary : Sixteen traditional stories retold by
award-winning author Jane Yolen.
ISBN 1-56397-484-3
1. Children's stories. 2. Folklore—Children's literature. 3. Short stories—Children's literature.
[1. Tales. 2. Folklore. 3. Short stories.]
I. Councell, Ruth Tietjen, ill. II. Title.
[E]—dc20 1997 AC CIP
Library of Congress Catalog Card Number 96-80397

First edition, 1997
Book designed by Jean Krulis
The text of this book is set in 14-point Garamond Light.
The illustrations are done in watercolors.

10 9 8 7 6 5 4 3 2

CONTENTS

THE THREE LITTLE PIGS

Once upon a time there was an old sow who had three little pigs. She loved those little pigs and kept them warm and fed. But they grew and grew, and she was so poor she could no longer keep them, so she sent them out into the world to seek their fortunes.

But before they left, she gave them each a clean hankie and a word of warning. "Look out," she said, "for the wolf at your door." Then, with her own hankie, she waved good-bye.

And they went trotting off down the road.

Now, the first little pig met a man with a bundle of straw. "Please, man," said the little pig, "give me that straw to make a house. I will give you my hankie in exchange." And as it was a beautiful hankie, the man did. The little pig stitched and sewed and patted and pushed the straw into shape, and soon he had a fine straw house.

"I like my straw house," said the little pig, and he went in and closed the door behind.

But pretty soon along came a wolf, and he knocked at the door. "Little pig, little pig, let me come in."

The little pig looked out of the straw window and saw the wolf and remembered what his mama had told him. "Not by the hair of my chinny-chin-chin."

The wolf's face got red and his ears stuck straight out. He drew himself up, tall as a tree. "Then," he said, "I'll huff. And I'll puff. And I'll blow your house down."

Then he huffed and he puffed and he blew the house down.

The little pig ran out the back door all the way to his brother's house.

Now, the second little pig had met a man with a bundle of sticks. "Please, man," said the little pig, "give me those sticks to make a house. I will give you my hankie in exchange." And as it was a beautiful hankie, the man did. The little pig hammered and sawed and shoved and shifted those sticks into shape, and soon he had a fine stick house.

"I like my stick house," said the little pig, and he went in and closed the door behind.

Just then there was a *rat-a-tat-tat* on the door, and when he opened it, there was his brother, sweaty and out of breath. He let his brother in.

"The wolf—" the first little pig had barely gotten out when the wolf was at the door.

"Little pig, little pig," said the wolf, "let me come in."

The little pig, remembering what his mama had said and seeing the state his brother was in, replied, "Not by the hair of my chinny-chin-chin."

The wolf's nose began to drip and the hairs on his tail got quite stiff. He drew himself up, tall as a tree. "Then," he said, "I'll huff. And I'll puff. And I'll blow your house down."

Then he huffed and he puffed and he blew the house down.

Both little pigs ran out the back door all the way to their brother's house.

Now, the third little pig had met a man with a load of bricks. "Please, man," said the little pig, "give me those bricks to build a house with and I will work for you this week." The man gave him the bricks and showed him the best way to build a house, and the little pig stacked and styled and laid those bricks the proper way, and eventually he had a fine brick house.

Pretty soon his brothers showed up, dazed and scared, and he let them in.

"The wolf—" they both gasped. So he gave them each some hot chocolate and put them to bed. And no sooner had he settled in his chair when there was a hard and hearty knock at the door.

"Little pig, little pig," called the wolf, "let me come in."

The little pig shook his head. "Not by the hair of my chinny-chin-chin."

The wolf's eyes grew squinty and his teeth ground together.

He drew himself up, tall as a tree. "Then," he said, "I'll huff. And I'll puff. And I'll blow your house down."

Well, he huffed.

And he puffed.

And he huffed.

And he puffed.

And he huffedandpuffedandhuffedandpuffed but he could *not* blow the house down. So he growled and yowled and moaned and groaned and decided then and there that he would climb down the chimney and get that little pig.

When the little pig heard wolf claws on his window, he wondered. When he heard wolf claws on his walls, he worried. But when he heard wolf claws going across his roof and over to his chimney, he knew just what to do. Still hanging over the blazing fire was the pot of water he had used to make his brothers' hot chocolate. So when he heard the wolf start down the chimney, he took the cover off the pot.

The wolf came down — *s p l a t* — right in the bubbling water, and it boiled the hair right off him. He screamed and howled and ran out the door. Then he moved way to the south, where he could be warm without his fur coat, and never bothered the pigs again.

And as for the three little pigs, they built a brick cottage next door for their mama, and they all lived happily ever after.

—a folktale from England

THE TORTOISE AND THE HARE

Once upon a time there was a hare who was proud of his speed. "I am the fastest runner in the land," he boasted to every creature he met.

In fact he boasted so much that the rest of the animals soon got tired of listening to him. But only one, the tortoise, decided to do anything about it.

"If you are so fast," Tortoise said, "prove it."

"What—against you?" Hare laughed. "You are the forest slowpoke. You are a laggard and a lugabout, a dawdler and a slug. I will have no problem beating you."

"Fast talk," retorted Tortoise, "is not fast walk."

"Name the place, lie-abed," Hare said.

So they fixed a time and place for a race and went their separate ways, Hare to his local diner where he laughed with his few friends, and Tortoise to practice running.

The day of the race was sunny. Frog had the starter gun and when it rang out, the race was begun.

Hare went galloping around the first bend, and when he saw that Tortoise had barely left the starting gate, he got a silly grin on his face.

"Tortoise is such a plodder, I will have time for a nap and will still lap him." So Hare lay down for a bit and was soon fast asleep.

Tortoise was a plodder indeed. But he put one foot steadily in front of another. When he came around the bend and saw Hare asleep, he tiptoed past. "You sleep and I'll slip by," he whispered, and he did just that.

The sun and Tortoise kept pace, and just at dusk Hare awoke. He looked behind him. No Tortoise.

He looked beside him. No Tortoise.

He looked ahead and—Tortoise! Tortoise was just about to cross the finish line.

Hare ran as fast as he could, which was very fast indeed. But he could not run fast enough. Tortoise crossed the finish line first and won the race.

"Slow and steady is the pace, slow and steady wins the race," said Tortoise.

All the other forest animals picked up that line and sang it long into the night.

And Hare went home, never to boast of his speed again.

—from Aesop

FINISH

THE SHOEMAKER AND THE ELVES

Once upon a time there was a poor shoemaker who became poorer every year. At last all he had left was leather enough for one pair of shoes.

"Wife, Wife, what shall I do?" he cried.

His wife shook her head. "You can do what you can do," she said. "Cut out the patterns this evening, then come to bed. We shall say our prayers and hope for the best."

So he cut out the patterns and they went to sleep.

In the morning he took out his needle and thread and went to sew the last pair of shoes. But what should he find but the shoes already sewn and standing toe to toe, heel to heel on his table. The shoemaker picked up the shoes and looked carefully. The work was better than anything he could ever do.

"Wife, Wife," he cried, "look at this."

They were marveling at the tiny stitches, so neat and even,

when a customer came into the shop. He was so pleased with the shoes that he paid far more than the usual price and left whistling at his bargain.

There was enough money for the shoemaker to buy leather for two more pairs of shoes and a little left over for bread and cheese for their evening meal.

"Do what you can do this evening," his wife advised. "Cut out the patterns, then come to bed. We shall say our prayers and hope for the best."

And the next morning it was the same. There were two pairs of shoes, each as well stitched and handsome as the first. The first two customers who came into the store paid far more than for an ordinary pair of shoes. This time there was enough money for leather for four pairs of shoes and a dinner of bread and cheese and meat and milk besides.

And so it went. Each night the shoemaker cut out the leather patterns, and the shoes were finished by magic in the morn.

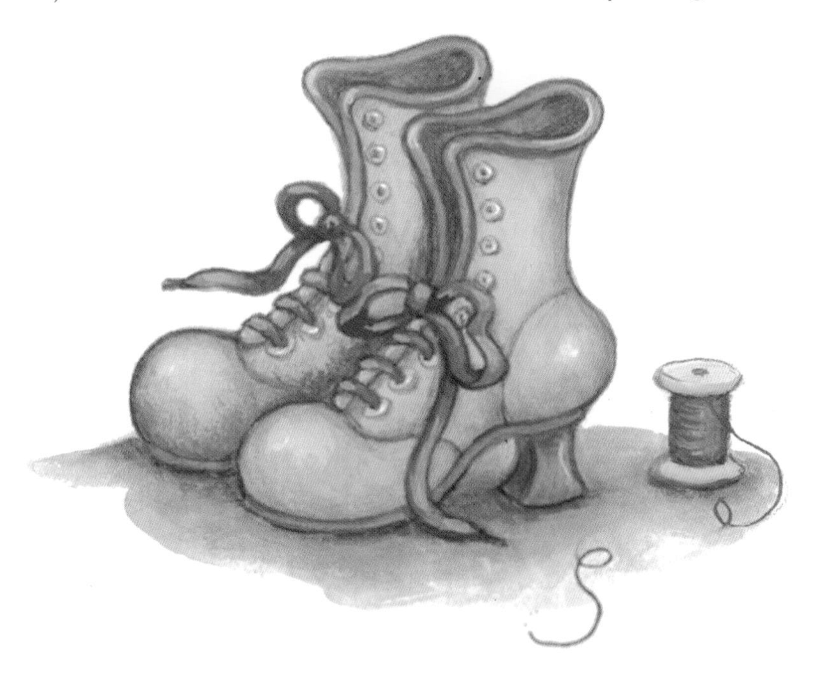

Customers were never lacking. Soon the shoemaker and his wife were rich beyond their dreams.

However, the shoemaker did not quite understand his good fortune. "Wife," he would say every morning, "is it a good spirit watching over us or an evil one?"

And she would answer, "Look at those stitches. So neat. So fine. Nothing wicked could sew such straight seams."

But one evening, right before Christmas, the shoemaker could stand the mystery no longer. "Let us go to bed as usual, Wife," he said. "But let us not fall asleep. That way we can find out who has been helping us these many months."

She agreed, for she was as curious as he. They cut out the patterns—for there was now so much work the wife had to help her husband. Then they said their prayers and went to bed.

But after a little while, they slipped out of bed and hid in a corner of the room to watch.

Just at midnight two tiny men, no bigger than the shoemaker's hand, came into the room and sat down on the shoemaker's table. They were as naked as newborns and did not speak. But, picking up the shoemaking tools, they got right to work. They hammered and nailed and stitched and sewed until the bell on the church tower chimed six times. Then they stood up, silently surveyed their work, and disappeared.

"Those little men have made us rich, Wife," the shoemaker said. "And yet they have nothing for themselves."

"Poor mites," the wife said. "They must be freezing in the cold. Now that we know who they are, I shall make them tiny

shirts and pants and coats, and you must make them each a pair of shoes. It will be our Christmas gifts to them. They have done so much for us."

So the shoemaker and his wife worked hard all that day, and by evening they had everything ready. They set out the gifts the way they set out the leather patterns on top of the table. Then they said their prayers and went to bed.

But right before midnight, they rose and hid in the corner.

The church bell struck the hour of twelve and in came the little men. They hopped up onto the table, prepared to do their night's work. But instead of leather, they found the wonderful clothes that the shoemaker and his wife had sewn for them.

The little men looked at each other in delight. They put on their little shirts and pants and coats. They buckled the tiny shoes on their feet. Then they turned and bowed to each other, laughing. They sang:

"See what handsome boys we are,
We will make those shoes no more."

They leaped and danced across the table, over the chairs, and out the door.

From that night to this, they never returned to the shoemaker's shop. But the good shoemaker and his wife continued to do well and they did, indeed, live happily ever after.

—from the Brothers Grimm

THREE BILLY GOATS GRUFF

Once upon a time there were three billy goats Gruff who lived in a good green meadow.

The smallest was Little Billy Goat Gruff, who was so small his horns were just nubbins.

The next was Middle Billy Goat Gruff, who was middle in everything. He was middle sized and middle weight and middle aged, too. He had horns just big enough to catch the light of the sun.

And the largest was Big Billy Goat Gruff. He was rough and tough and had horns as sharp as gaff hooks.

Alongside their good green meadow was a wide, swift river. On the other side of this river was a meadow, even greener than the one in which they lived. But they never dared cross over the bridge to that other side because long ago their mama had warned them that under the bridge lived a troll. And—as everybody knows—there is nothing trolls like better for dinner than billy goats Gruff.

One day the sun shone down on the other meadow and made it look so green and sweet and tempting that all three billy goats Gruff sighed. They wanted to eat that grass more than anything in the world.

At last Little Billy Goat Gruff spoke up. "I am going across the bridge to that meadow and eat that grass, and I am going right now."

"Oh, no!" his brothers warned. "Remember about the troll!"

Little Billy Goat Gruff shook his head, the one with the horns that were just nubbins. "I have never seen a troll," he said. "And what I don't see, I don't believe." He put his little hooves on the bridge and started across.

Trit-trot, trit-trot, trit-trit, trot-trot, trit-trot . . . till he was halfway.

And suddenly, up from under the bridge came . . .

THE TROLL.

The troll was nine feet tall and he was nine feet wide. He was mean and he was green. He had a nose like a banana. He had ears like leaves. He had teeth like knives. And he was very, very ugly.

"Ho-ho-ho-ho-ho-ho-ho-ho," said the troll. "I smell dinner."

Little Billy Goat Gruff squeaked. "Dinner? Me? But . . . ," and he began to speak very fast. "But I am just a very little billy goat Gruff. And if you ate me, one bite and I would be gone and you would still be hungry. But . . . ," and he took a deep breath. "But if you wait for my older brother, Middle Billy Goat Gruff, to come along, you will have a meal fit for a king."

Now, trolls may be mean. And trolls may be green. But trolls are also very, very stupid!

The troll said, "Duh . . . you are just a little goat?"

"Very little."

"And one bite, you'd be gone?"

"Quite gone."

"But if I wait till your older brother comes along, I will have a meal fit for a king?"

"Fit for a king troll," said Little Billy Goat Gruff.

The troll thought about this for as long as a stupid troll can think. And then at last he said, "Well, run along, run along, run along."

And *trit-trot, trit-trot, trit-trit-trot,* Little Billy Boat Gruff went over the bridge to the other side, where he ate that good green grass till his belly got as big and as round as a drum.

But—meanwhile—Middle Billy Goat Gruff suddenly looked up and over and saw his little brother safe and happy in the green meadow on the other side. "Well . . . ," he said.

"Well what?" asked his older brother.

"I am going across the bridge to the other side," said Middle

Billy Goat Gruff, "so I can eat the good green grass till my tummy gets as big and as round as a drum."

"Oh, no," said Big Billy Goat Gruff. "What about that troll?"

Middle Billy Goat Gruff shook his head, the one with the horns just big enough to catch the light of the sun. "I have never seen a troll," he said. "And what I don't see, I don't believe." And he put his middle-sized hooves on the bridge and started across.

Trit-trot, trit-trot, trit-trit, trot-trot, trit-trot . . . till he was halfway.

And suddenly, up from under the bridge came . . .

THE TROLL.

The troll was nine feet tall and he was nine feet wide. He was mean and he was green. He had a nose like a banana. He had ears like leaves. He had teeth like knives. And he was very, very ugly.

"Ho-ho-ho-ho-ho, ha-ha-ha-ha-ha," said the troll. "I smell dinner."

Middle Billy Goat Gruff squealed. "Dinner? Me? But . . . ," and he began to speak very fast. "I am just middle sized and middle weight," he said. "If you ate me—one bite, then two—I would be gone and you would still be hungry. But . . . ," and he took a very deep breath. "But if you wait for my older brother, Big Billy Goat Gruff, to come along, you will have a meal fit for a king."

Now, you must remember—trolls are very, very stupid.

The troll said, "Duh . . . you are just a middle-sized goat?"

"Less than middle sized, actually."

"And one bite, two, and you'd be gone?"

"Entirely gone."

"But if I wait till your older brother comes along, I will have a meal fit for a king?"

"Fit for a king troll," said Middle Billy Goat Gruff.

The troll thought about this for about as long as a stupid troll can think. And then at last he said, "Well, run along, run along, run along."

And *trit-trot, trit-trot, trit-trit-trot,* Middle Billy Goat Gruff went over the bridge to the other side, where he ate the good green grass till his belly got as big and as round as a drum.

But—meanwhile—Big Billy Goat Gruff looked up suddenly and saw his two younger brothers safe and happy in the green meadow on the other side. *Well,* he thought. "And well . . . ," he said aloud, though there was no one left to argue with him. "Besides," he said, "I have never seen a troll, and what I don't see, I don't believe." And he put his big hooves on the bridge and started across.

Trit-trot, trit-trot, trit-trit, trot-trot, trit-trot . . . till he was halfway.

And suddenly, up from under the bridge came . . .

THE TROLL.

The troll was nine feet tall and he was nine feet wide. He was mean and he was green. He had a nose like a banana. He had ears like leaves. He had teeth like knives. And he was very, very ugly.

"Ho-ho-ho-ho-ho-ho-ho-ho-ho, ha-ha-ha-ha-ha-ha-ha-ha-ha, he-he-he-he-he-he-he-he-he," said the troll. "I smell dinner. And, BOY, am I hungry!"

Big Billy Goat Gruff looked at the troll out of the corner of his eye and measured him up and down before speaking. And then he said, "If you are thinking of eating me for dinner, you are a troll of exceptional taste."

The troll said, "Duh—I am?"

"You certainly are," said Big Billy Goat Gruff. "I will make a great meal. I will make excellent Gruff Burgers, terrific goat stew, amazing T-goat steak, and sensational Billy Pizza."

The troll looked even hungrier than before.

"But how are you going to eat me?" asked Big Billy Goat Gruff.

"With my mouth," said the troll. "With my mouth. I am not going to put you in my ear. I am not going to put you in my nose. I am going to put you in my mouth." And if you think this is an extremely stupid conversation, remember that trolls are extremely stupid, indeed.

"That is good," said Big Billy Goat Gruff. "Because in the ear is silly. And up the nose is gross. But putting me in your mouth is the reasonable and polite way to eat." He smiled at the troll and waggled his head, and only an extremely stupid troll would not then have noticed the horns as large as gaff hooks. "But I am afraid your mouth is too small for such a big billy goat as I."

The troll opened his mouth wide . . . and w i d e . . . and *w i d e r* still.

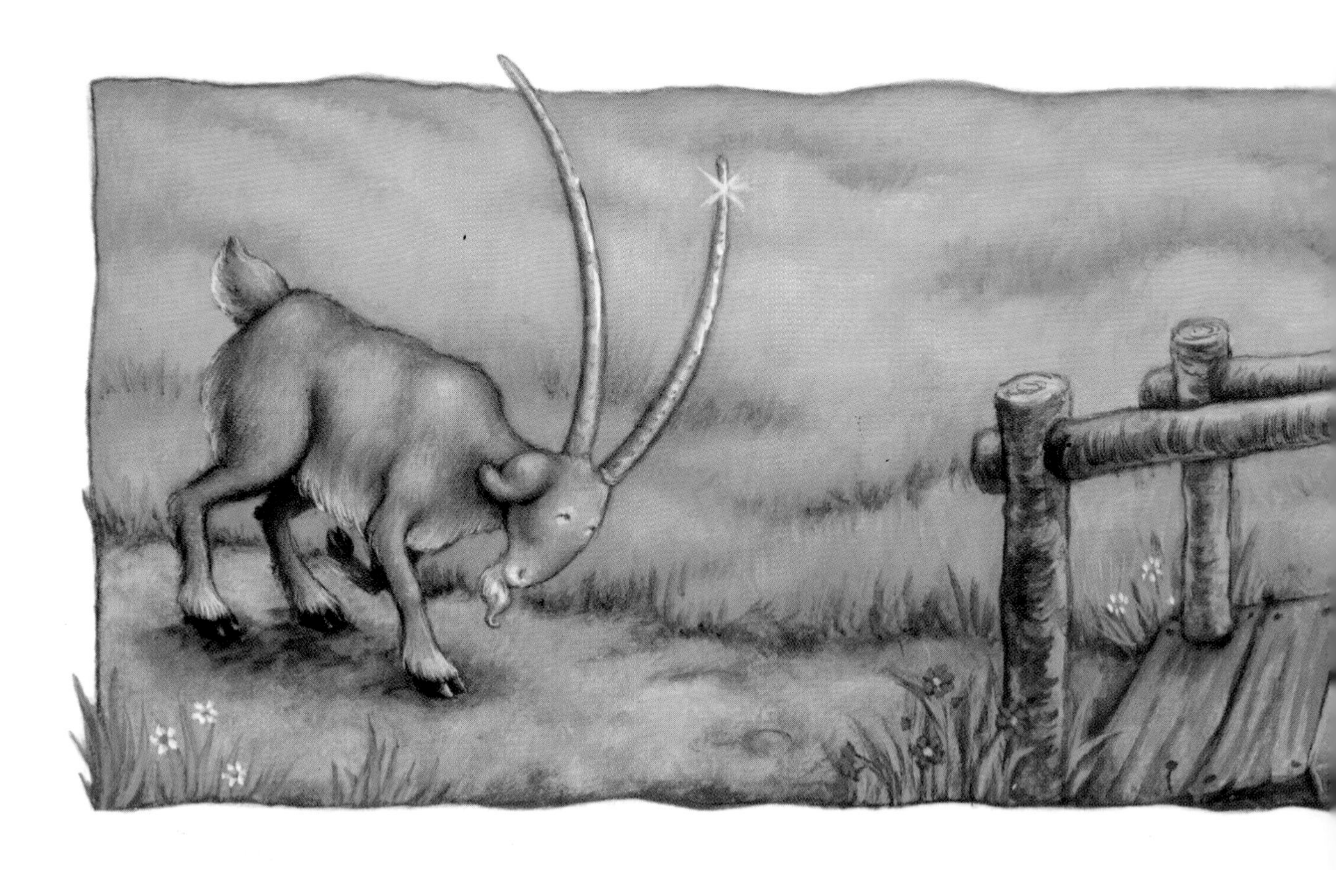

"Not big enough," said Big Billy Goat Gruff. "But you seem a nice enough troll, and so I am willing to help you. Listen carefully and do as I say."

The troll nodded, closed his mouth, opened his ears, and listened.

"You are going to squat right there in the middle of the bridge and open your mouth as wide as you possibly can. And I am going to back up to the beginning of the bridge, take a running start, and leap right down your throat," said Big Billy Goat Gruff. "And you won't even have to chew."

So that's what they did. The troll squatted on the bridge and opened his big mouth as *w i d e* as it would go. And Big Billy

Goat Gruff backed up till he was at the beginning of the bridge. He put his great head down so that the horns as sharp as gaff hooks were pointed right at the troll's belly. Then pawing the ground three times, Big Billy Goat Gruff began to run.

He ran and he ran and he ran and he ran until his horns went—*bam*—right into the troll's belly and lifted him high into the air. Then the troll went flying up and up and up above the river, and then down, and down, and down, and—*splat*—into the river. He floated away downstream and was never seen again.

As for Big Billy Goat Gruff, he went *trit-trot, trit-trot, trit-trit-trot* all the way across the bridge, where he joined his two brothers in the other meadow. They ate and ate until their bellies were as big and as tight as drums, and they waddled back to the other side. And there they lived happily ever after in the good green grass. For all I know, they may be there still.

—*a folktale from Norway*

TALK

Once long ago in Africa, a farmer went out to his garden to dig up some yams to sell at the market. It was a hot day, but not too hot, and so he dug away with his digging stick with great vigor.

While he was digging, one of the yams cried out, "Go away, dirt man. You never bothered to weed me and never bothered to feed me, and now you come to dig me up."

Well, the man was so amazed he turned to see who was speaking, but all that was behind him was his cow chewing her cud. "Cow, was that you?"

The cow, being a cow, kept on chewing. But the man's dog spoke up.

"It wasn't the cow that spoke," the dog said. "It was the yam. And yam says to leave him alone, dirt man."

The man threw down his digging stick and stomped his foot,

furious because his dog had never spoken to him before, and besides, he didn't like the dog's tone. "I will show you who is a dirt man," he said, and he took out his knife and cut a branch from the palm tree to whip his dog.

The palm tree said, "Put that branch down."

The man was really upset now, the way things were going, and he started to throw the branch away angrily.

But the palm branch said, "Man, put me down gently, gently."

Frightened, the man placed the branch gently on a stone.

The stone said, "Hey, don't put that thing on me."

This was too much, and the man ran away, heading toward his

village. On the way he met a fisherman with a fish trap balanced on his head.

"What's the hurry?" asked the fisherman.

"What's the hurry? You would hurry, too, if you had heard what I heard," said the man. "My yam said 'Leave me alone.' My dog said 'Leave him alone.' The tree said 'Put the branch down.' The branch said 'Gently, gently.'" He wiped his sweating forehead. "And the stone told me not to put the branch on him."

"And is that so frightening?" asked the fisherman.

"And did you take the branch off the stone?" asked the fish trap on the fisherman's head.

"Wah! Wah!" screamed the fisherman, and he flung down the fish trap. And the two of them—fisherman and farmer—ran down the road.

They ran until they came to a weaver with a bundle of cloth balanced on his head.

"What's the hurry?" he called out to them.

"You would hurry, too, if you had heard what we heard," said the fisherman.

"My yam said 'Leave me alone,'" said the farmer. "My dog said 'Leave him alone.' The tree said 'Put the branch down.' The branch said 'Gently, gently.' And the stone told me not to put the branch on him."

"And then," the fisherman added, "my fish trap said 'Did he take the branch off the stone?'"

"That is nothing to get excited about," said the weaver, "not that I can see."

"Oh, yes, it is," said the bundle of cloth on the weaver's head, "if it happened to you."

"Wah! Wah!" the weaver cried and flung his bundle on the trail. And then the three of them—farmer and fisherman and weaver—ran down the road.

They ran and ran and ran until they came to the village and ran down the main street to the house of the chief. The chief's servant brought a stool out, and out came the chief to sit on his stool and listen to the men's complaints.

The men began to tell their tale.

"I went out into my garden," said the farmer, "to dig up my

yam. And my yam began to talk. And my dog began to talk. And the palm tree and the palm-tree branch and the stone all began to talk."

The fisherman added, "And then my fish trap began to talk."

And the weaver added, "And so did my bundle of cloth."

The chief listened to them patiently until they were done. Then he shook his head. "This is a bad story," he said, "and difficult to believe. You had better go back to your work before I have to punish you for disturbing the peace."

So the men had to go away, and the chief shook his head again. "Such nonsense," he said out loud. "A story like that could upset the whole village."

"Fantastic!" agreed his stool. "Imagine—a talking yam!"

—a folktale from the Ashanti people, Africa

THE SNOW CHILD

Once upon a time in a faraway village in Russia there lived an old farmer and his wife. They had a snug little house and a fine farm. There were ducks and hens in the yard and a big brown cow that gave the sweetest milk.

But they had no children and this made them very sad, for they wanted children more than anything in the world.

One cold winter morning, the farmer's wife went to take a cake to her neighbor when she saw that the village children had made snowmen and snow women all along the walks. And without quite knowing why, she put down the cake and began to roll a ball of snow.

"What are you doing?" her husband asked, for he was off to the forest to cut some firewood.

"I am going to make a little snow child," she said, "a little girl. She shall stand outside our house and smile at us when we go out and when we come in."

And because he knew how much his wife wanted a child—even a snow child—the farmer put down his ax and helped her with the snow.

They rolled and patted and sculpted the prettiest little snow girl you can imagine. She wore a white dress and had a sweet, curved snow smile.

"Oh," the farmer's wife said. "She is such a dear. If only she were real."

"But I *am* real!" a tiny voice said, right from the snow.

And sure enough, there she was—a little girl with white-gold hair and blue-white eyes, laughing and holding her hands up to them.

"She is a *snegurochka*, a winter child," said the farmer. "I have heard of them."

The farmer's wife cried, "Oh, will you stay with us and be our daughter?"

"I will be your daughter gladly," said the snow child.

So happy was the old woman that when she hugged the snow girl, the old woman did not mind how cold the girl was or notice that she had answered only half the question.

They brought the snow child into the house, and the old woman set dinner before her. But the child would take nothing but a glass of cold milk. And she would not sit on the bench by the fire. Instead, she moved next to the window and opened it to breathe in the icy air.

"Are you comfortable there in the cold, my child?" asked the farmer.

"I am comfortable indeed," said the child. "You must not let me get too warm, you know. I am, after all, made of snow."

The old woman smiled. "I know, I know," she said. But she hardly remembered it. "I shall make you a bed and tuck you in, for it is long past your bedtime. And I shall make you a dozen pretty dresses. And Papa will get you new boots."

"No, my dear mama," the girl said, "my snow dress is the finest dress I shall wear. And I dare not sleep in your bed. I will be better outside in the snow." She went to the door and started to open it.

"But you promised . . . ," they both cried.

"I shall be your daughter," the snow child said. "But I must sleep in the snow." And out she went. There she lay down beside the house and in a minute was fast asleep.

The farmer and his wife stared at her from the door. Then at last the farmer said, "Tomorrow I shall build her a proper bed so she does not have to sleep on the ground."

The very next day he was as good as his word. He built an open porch with a bed and a chair and a table and even a toy box of the finest ash, which he filled with toys.

The farmer's wife made cold soups and ice creams for their daughter to eat.

Often they would look up from their work to see the snow girl playing with the other children in the village, her white dress and white-gold hair blowing in the wind.

It was the happiest winter any of them could recall.

But soon enough the days grew warmer. The snow girl spent more and more time quietly resting in her bed on the open porch. She no longer ran and sang with the other children.

"Are you sick, my child?" asked the farmer's wife.

"Just tired, Mama," the child answered.

"Are you ill, my daughter?" asked the farmer.

"I have played too hard all winter," she replied.

And then one day, when the last of the snow was melting on the faraway mountains, she cried out to them. "Mama, Papa, I must go away."

The farmer's wife sat by her, tears in her eyes. "But you

promised you would be our daughter and stay with us always."

"I said I would be your little girl," the snow child said. "I did not promise I could stay."

The old couple began to weep loudly.

But the child held their hands. "When the first snow comes again, make a snow girl," she said. "And I shall come back and be your winter daughter."

"Do you promise?" they asked, holding her cold hands in theirs.

"I promise gladly," she said in a thin little voice. And then she melted away, and there was nothing left but a small silver puddle by the bed.

Spring and summer were hard on the old farmer and his wife. They remembered the laughter of their little snow child, and it was difficult to believe that she would return.

But winter came again soon enough. The first snows fell in October. And as soon as there was enough on the ground, the farmer and his wife went outside and rolled a ball of snow. Then they patted and sculpted it into the very image of their snow daughter.

With the final pat on the head, they heard a tiny, silvery laugh.

"Mama, Papa," cried the snow child. "I am home!"

—a folktale from Russia

THE PRINCESS AND THE PEA

Once upon a time there was a prince who wanted more than anything to marry. But he had to marry a *real* princess—and there was the problem. Though he went all around the world meeting one lovely girl after another, there was always something not quite right.

"They just aren't *real* princesses," he said to his mother and father when he returned.

"What is a *real* princess?" asked his father, the king.

"He will know her when he sees her," said his mother, the queen. "After all, dear, you knew when you met me."

And they smiled at each other fondly, which made the prince even more miserable than before.

Now, one evening a great storm broke over the kingdom. Lightning lit the sky and rain came down in barrelfuls. All the people for miles around stayed inside and shivered by their fires.

Suddenly there was a knock on the palace door, and the king himself went to answer it.

Outside stood a princess, but—heavens!—how drenched she was. Her hair was so wet it was hard to see its color. Streams of water ran through her clothes, flowing down into the heels of her shoes and out through the toes.

"Who are you?" asked the king.

"I am a princess," she said.

"A princess?" the prince said as he looked up, but it was hard to see if she was a *real* princess through all that wetness.

"Never mind," said his mother. "We will find out soon enough." And she hurried to a palace guest room and took off all the sheets and blankets from the bed. Then on that mattress she placed a tiny pea. She remade the bed and then put twenty mattresses from the other guest rooms on top of it. Then she put twenty quilts on top of them.

"Come, my dear," she said to the princess, leading her to the room. "I have made up the bed especially for you."

The princess needed a ladder to get to the top, but she was so tired she went right to bed.

In the morning the king, the queen, and the prince waited in the breakfast room for the princess to appear.

When she came in, she was dry and beautiful. Her hair was the black of deepest night, her eyes the color of the ground after rain. But she was not smiling.

"How did you sleep, my dear?" asked the queen.

The princess rolled her earth-brown eyes to the heavens. "I do not want to complain," she said. "But I had a wretched night. There was something small and hard in the bed, and it has quite bruised me all over."

"All over?" asked the queen.

"All over?" asked the king and prince.

"All over," said the princess.

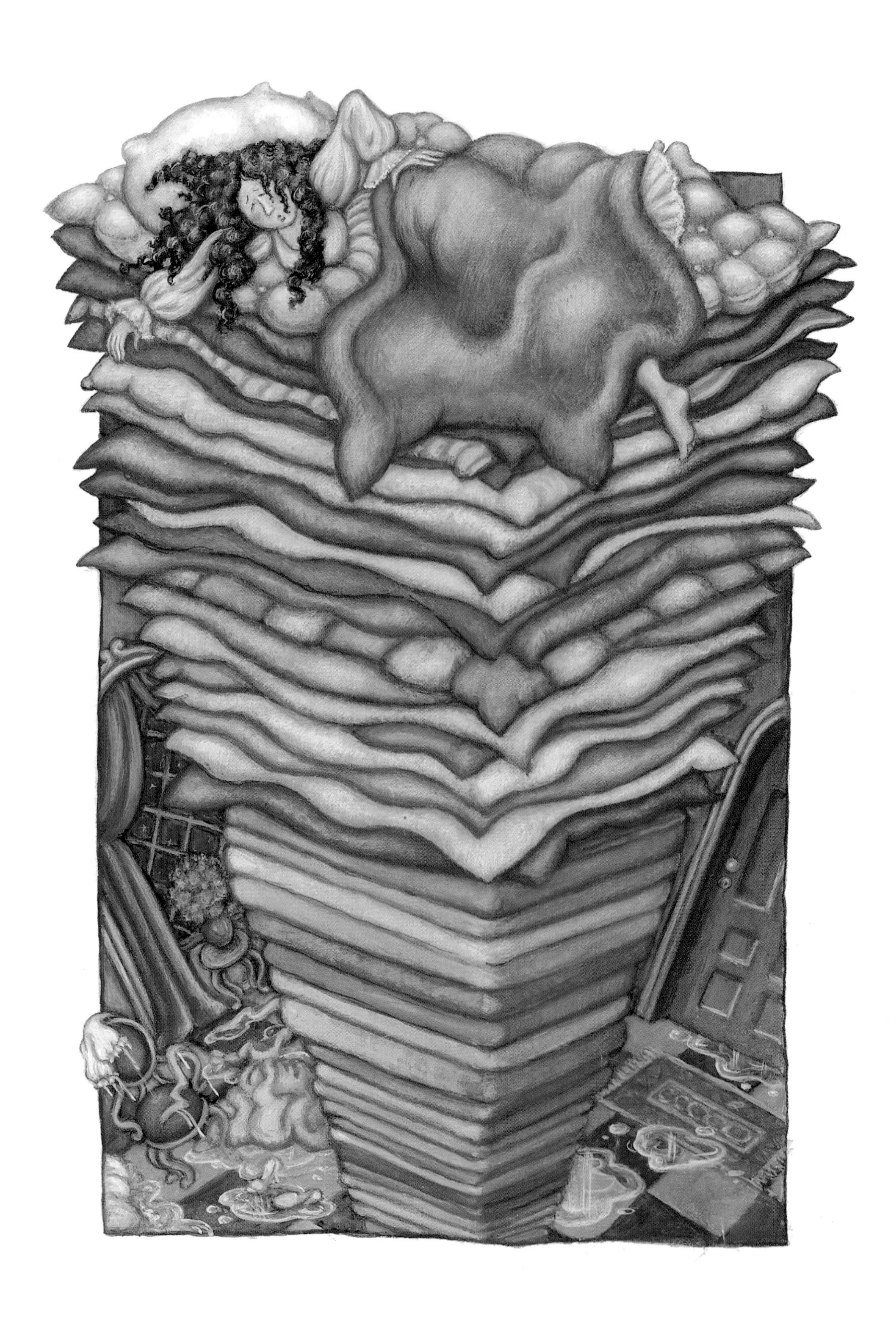

"Hurrah!" cried the queen, "you are a *real* princess indeed. For who but a *real* princess could feel a pea through twenty mattresses and twenty quilts?"

So the prince married her. And the pea was exhibited for years in the royal museum. You can go and see it yourself—if it hasn't shriveled to nothing.

—from Hans Christian Andersen

THE THREE BEARS

Once upon a time in a cottage in the forest lived a family of three bears.

There was Papa Bear, who was a great **big** bear.

And there was Mama Bear, who was a middle-sized bear.

And Baby Bear, who was just a wee little thing.

They each had a bowl for their porridge. Papa Bear's bowl was a great **big** thing. Mama Bear's bowl was middling. And Baby Bear's bowl was a tiny wee thing. But how they all loved their porridge.

They each had a chair to sit in. Papa Bear's chair was a great **big** thing. Mama Bear's chair was middling. And Baby Bear's chair was a tiny wee thing. But how they loved to sit in them.

And they each had a bed to sleep in. Papa Bear's bed was a great **big** thing. Mama Bear's bed was middling. And Baby Bear's bed was a tiny wee thing. But how they loved to sleep in them.

Now one day, after they had made porridge and poured it into their bowls, the three bears decided to go for a walk in the woods to let the porridge cool. They were three very smart bears, and they did not want to burn their tongues by eating porridge that was too hot. While they were out walking on the east road, who should come by the west road but a curious little girl named Goldilocks, who had sneaked away from her house when her mother wasn't looking.

Seeing the three bears' cottage, she peeked into the window. As there was no one inside, she lifted the latch on the door and walked right in.

Oh, no!

Goldilocks tossed her golden curls. She sniffed. Something wonderful-smelling was on the table. She went right over and saw it was the porridge.

Goldilocks loved porridge. So she picked up a spoon and ate a bit from the great **big** bowl. But it was too hot.

Ouch!

So she ate a bit from the middling bowl. But it was too cold.

Pooh!

So she tried a bit from the tiny wee bowl. It was just right. So she ate it up, every last bit.

Oh, no!

Then because she had walked a long way to get to the three bears' house, she thought she might sit down. So she sat in the great **big** chair. But it was too hard.

Ouch!

So she sat down in the middling chair. But it was too soft.

Pooh!

So she sat down in the tiny wee chair. It was just right. So she rocked and rocked and rocked and rocked until she rocked it all to pieces!

Oh, no!

Well, she was so tired from her adventure that she went upstairs to the bedroom and saw three beds all in a row.

She climbed onto the great **big** bed. But it was too high at the head.

Ouch!

So she climbed into the middling bed. But that was too high at the foot.

Pooh!

So she lay on the tiny wee bed. It was just right. So she pulled the quilt up to her chin, closed her eyes, and went right to sleep.

Oh, no!

By this time the three bears thought their porridge would be cool enough, and so they came home to breakfast.

Papa Bear took one look at his porridge bowl and knew something was wrong.

"SOMEBODY HAS EATEN MY PORRIDGE!" he cried in his big-bear voice.

Mama Bear took one look at her porridge bowl and knew something was wrong.

"SOMEBODY HAS EATEN MY PORRIDGE!" she cried in her middling-bear voice.

Baby Bear took one look at his porridge bowl and knew something was wrong.

"Somebody has eaten my porridge," he cried in his tiny wee-bear voice, "and gobbled it all up!"

Knowing someone had been in the house, the three bears looked around them.

Papa Bear went over to his chair and saw the cushions were all this way and that.

"SOMEBODY HAS BEEN SITTING IN MY CHAIR!" he cried in his big-bear voice.

Mama Bear went over to her chair and saw that the cushions were all this way and that.

"SOMEBODY HAS BEEN SITTING IN MY CHAIR!" she cried in her middling-bear voice.

Baby Bear went over to his chair and saw that the cushions were all this way and that—and the arms and legs and rockers as well. "Somebody has been sitting in my chair," he cried in his tiny wee-bear voice, "and rocked it all to pieces!"

The three bears began to growl, and they searched around the rest of the house and at last went up the stairs to check the bedroom.

Papa Bear took one look at his bed with the pillows all this way and that.

"SOMEBODY HAS BEEN SLEEPING IN MY BED!" he cried in his big-bear voice.

Mama Bear took one look at her bed with the pillows all this way and that.

"SOMEBODY HAS BEEN SLEEPING IN MY BED!" she cried in her middling-bear voice.

Baby Bear looked at his bed and saw the covers were all pulled about and the pillows were all this way and that. "Somebody has been sleeping in my bed," he cried in his tiny wee-bear voice. "And here she is!"

Just then Goldilocks woke up and saw the three bears standing over her, and they did not look very happy. She jumped out of

bed, climbed out the window, scurried down a vine, and ran home, where her mama gave her a talking-to for running away—and you can believe it was a rough one. And she never went back to the three bears' house again.

—from Robert Southey and the English folktale tradition

THE EMPEROR'S NEW CLOTHES

Once upon a time in a far-off land there was an emperor who was so fond of new clothes that he spent all his money on them. He had a new outfit for every hour of the day. And if he hadn't been such a nice emperor, his people might have hated him for it. But as it was they just laughed and said in a kindly fashion, "Well, he might have been spending that money on wars."

One day two bad men came into the town. They told everyone they were weavers who could weave the most wonderful cloth. They said that the cloth was of the finest and rarest silken threads. But best of all, they said, the cloth was invisible to anyone who was unfit for his office or who was extremely stupid.

Now, you or I would know that these men were liars and trying to swindle everyone in the kingdom. But in those days, people really believed that things could become invisible, and so they thought the two men were telling the truth.

The emperor thought they were telling the truth, too. And he thought, *If I had robes made of this marvelous cloth, I would know which of my councilors were unfit for office and which of my people were extremely stupid.* So he sent for the two men and gave them a lot of money so that they would make him new clothes from their wonderful cloth.

The two men set up a loom in the royal fitting room and pretended they were working. They sang as they worked, a song that went something like this:

> *"Watch us weave, watch us sew,*
> *If you can't see this, then we know*
> *You are stupid, you are dumb,*
> *You don't know your elbow from your thumb."*

The emperor really wanted to know how the two weavers were getting along, but he was a little nervous to go see for himself. *What would happen,* he wondered, *if I could not see the cloth? Then everyone would know I am unfit to be emperor.* So instead he sent his faithful prime minister.

Now, the prime minister was a sweet old man who was loyal to the emperor and loved his work. But when he went into the fitting room and saw the empty loom and the two swindlers pretending to weave, his heart skipped a beat. He closed his eyes and opened them again, but the loom was still empty. *Heaven preserve me!* he thought. *I cannot see a thing. I must be unfit for my office. Or else I am extremely stupid.* But he said nothing about this out loud.

"Well," the swindlers said, "Prime Minister, what do you think? Is this not the loveliest cloth?" They knew he was too afraid to admit there was nothing to be seen.

And, indeed, the good old man stepped closer and examined the empty loom, saying, "My, my, my—what patterns! What colors! I shall tell the emperor how beautiful it is."

"And tell the emperor as well that if we are to finish in time for the great parade, we will need another payment at once."

"At once!" the prime minister agreed and hurried away. He told the emperor about the beautiful cloth and the emperor smiled. His prime minister was perfectly fit for his office and not stupid in the least.

The next day the emperor sent two more councilors to view

the cloth; the day after, three. And each time everyone agreed that, indeed, the cloth was the most beautiful in all the land.

At last the emperor himself went into the room where the weavers were working away furiously at their empty loom.

Behind the emperor came the prime minister and the rest of the councilors.

"Isn't it amazing?" said the prime minister.

"What magnificent colors," said half the councilors.

"What magnificent patterns," said the others.

Oh, dear, thought the emperor, *it is worse than I thought. I cannot see a thing. I am the only one in this entire room unfit for my position. I must be extremely stupid.* But he did not dare say anything aloud. Instead, he gave the two swindlers another pocketful of gold. "Enough weaving," he said. "Make the cloth into a suit of clothes that I can wear in the great parade tomorrow."

That night the two swindlers did not sleep at all. They had twenty candles lighting the room so everyone could see how busy they were. They pretended to take cloth from the loom. They cut the air with big scissors—*snip-snap.* And they sewed with needles that hadn't any thread.

When dawn arose, they got up and announced, "The emperor's clothes are ready."

The emperor came into the room, and the swindlers proceeded to help him into his new invisible clothes.

"First the pants, Your Majesty," said one.

"Now your shirt, Your Majesty," said the other.

"Now the coat," they said together.

The emperor stood in front of the mirror, admiring the clothes he could not see. Then he walked outside.

"Oh, how your new clothes suit you," everyone cried, because no one wanted to admit they could not see the cloth. No one wanted to be thought unfit or extremely stupid.

And so the parade began. Soldiers on horseback trotted ahead.

Then came the royal cannons pulled by oxen.

Then, the prime minister and the councilors.

And at last, the emperor himself, under a royal blue canopy held by four lovely young women.

All the people of the town, who had lined the streets or were looking down from their windows, cried out, "Look at the emperor's beautiful new clothes. Oh, how his new clothes suit him." For none of them wanted to admit that they could see nothing and were therefore unfit for their offices or extremely stupid.

"But he doesn't have anything on!" cried a little child, pointing as the emperor went by.

"Who said that?" asked the emperor. "WHO SAID THAT?" he roared.

The little child was pushed forward. "You don't have anything on," the child repeated.

And then the emperor knew, because the child was only a child after all, with no office to be unfit for. And no child can be extremely stupid, being young and innocent.

"I am not wearing anything at all," the emperor said out loud. "I am—in fact—naked. Oh, dear. Oh, dear."

And the prime minister took off his own robe of office and put it around the emperor, and they continued the parade that way till they went all around the town and back into the castle.

The emperor never overspent on new clothes again. And as for the swindlers, well, they got clear away and have never been heard of again from that time to this.

—*from Hans Christian Andersen*

THE LION AND THE MOUSE

Once upon a time in far-off Africa, a great lion was dozing sleepily on a rock in the sun. He was proud, but all lions are proud. He was handsome, but all lions are handsome. And he snored.

Suddenly a little mouse, scared and lost, bumped against the lion's nose and woke him.

Without even thinking—lions rarely think—the lion reached out with his great paw and imprisoned the mouse in his claws.

"Oh, oh, oh," squeaked the mouse, who was now more frightened than before, "please forgive me, Your Most Glorious Majesty."

The lion was flattered, but all lions are easily flattered.

"I know," the mouse continued, "that you could squish me and squash me with one little twist of your paw."

The lion smiled and showed his teeth. All lions show their teeth when they smile.

It did not make the mouse any less frightened. But mice, though small, are very smart. And she continued speaking. "How noble and glorious would it be, Your Magnificence, if you squished and squashed an insignificant mouse such as I?"

"And why should I show you any particular mercy?" asked the lion. "I mean, you did wake me up, after all."

"Well," the mouse said quietly, so quietly the lion had to put his great head right down next to his paw to hear. "Well, it would be noble of you to act with mercy. And perhaps one day, even such a small and miserable creature as I could do you a good turn. Who knows?"

"Ho! Ho! Ho!" The lion laughed so loudly he nearly blew the tail off the mouse. "That's a good one. A mouse helping a lion."

"If I can, I will," the mouse said.

"Don't push it, mouse," cautioned the lion. But he said it softly. "And be careful where you are running. Next time I might not want to be so . . . so noble." He opened his paw and the mouse ran out.

"Oh, thank you, Your Majesty," cried the mouse. But the lion did not hear her. He was already asleep and snoring in the hot summer sun.

Now a little while after, a week or maybe two, the lion was roaming around the forest and not really watching where he was going. Lions rarely watch where they are going. They are kings of the jungle, after all.

So the lion walked right into a net, a net set out by hunters who wanted a lion to take back to a zoo. The lion roared and roared, but it did no good. He was tangled tight. A net has no ears for hearing and no heart for pity.

Many of the animals in the forest heard the lion roar, but none wanted to help him except the little mouse. She was quietly eating some seeds when she heard his cry.

"Ah," she said to herself, "a promise is a promise, whether big or small." She set down the seeds and ran to the place where the lion was caught in the net.

"As you took pity on me, Your Majesty, so I will take pity on you." She gnawed on the net until she made a hole large enough for the lion to get through.

From that day to this, the lion has been mindful of small creatures.

And the mouse? Well, she is still careful where she goes running. Mice are smart animals, after all.

—from Aesop

STONE SOUP

Once upon a time three weary soldiers trudged down a road—hup and one, hup and two. They were on their way home from the wars and had not eaten in days. Oh, they were hungry.

Suddenly they could see the lights of a village ahead.

"Maybe," said the first soldier, "we can find something to eat there."

"Something big," said the second soldier.

"And a place to sleep as well," said the third.

So—hup and one, hup and two—they hurried along the road.

Now, the people who lived in that village feared strangers. And after so many years of war, they especially feared soldiers. So when they saw three soldiers hurrying down the road, the villagers quickly agreed to hide all their food.

"For we have barely enough for ourselves," said the mayor.

They hid sacks of barley under the hay.

They lowered buckets of milk down the wells.

They covered carrots and potatoes, cabbages and beans. They hung the meat away in the cellars. And then they waited for the soldiers to arrive.

Hup and one, hup and two—the soldiers stopped at the first house.

"Please," they said, "could you spare a bit to eat for three hungry men?"

"We have no food," said the farmer and his wife. "See for yourselves. It has been a bad harvest."

The soldiers went on to the next house. "Can you feed three hungry men?" they asked.

"Nothing here. Nothing to spare," said the farmer and his wife.

And so it went throughout the entire village. There was not one bit of food to be found.

The three soldiers understood all too well what war can do. So they stood in the middle of the town square. "Good people," they called out, "we know you have no food to give us. So we would like to make food for you. We will make you Stone Soup."

STONE SOUP? No one in the village had ever heard of that. Not even Madame Danton, who was the best cook of all.

"This I should like to see," said a farmer to his wife.

"That you shall," said the soldiers. "But first we will need a large pot to cook it in."

"I have such a pot," said Madame Danton. And she sent her strong sons to bring it out.

The Danton boys rolled the huge pot into the square.

"Now," said the first soldier, "we will need water to fill it and a fire to heat it."

"I will fetch water," said one farmer.

"And I, wood," said another. And they quickly got what they had promised.

Soon the fire was burning merrily, and the water in the pot began to boil.

"And now," said the second soldier, "we will need three round, clean stones."

Well, those were easy enough to find. And one! Two! Three! The stones were dropped into the pot. "Ah . . . ," said the soldiers, sniffing the air appreciatively.

"Of course," the third soldier said, "the soup will improve with a little salt and pepper."

"Of course," said Madame Danton.

And off went three children to fetch them.

"As good as Stone Soup is," the soldiers said together, "it always improves with some carrots."

"Why, I think I may have a single carrot," said a farmer's wife.

"And I another," said her husband.

They came back with almost a dozen carrots that had been hidden under their bed.

The first soldier took a long spoon and tasted the soup. "Very good," he said, "though it would be better yet with cabbage. But as we have none . . ."

"I may have a cabbage somewhere," said another farmer's wife.

"Or two," said her husband.

Husband and wife hurried away and came back with three they had put away under their bed.

The cabbages followed the carrots into the Stone Soup. This time the second soldier took the long spoon and tasted it. "Better and better," he said. "But if we had some potatoes and a bit of beef, why, this soup would be good enough for a rich man's table."

Well, wouldn't you know, some potatoes were found under another bed. And some beef. And some beans and barley as well. The villagers brought the food from the hidden places and put them in the soup.

The third soldier took the spoon and tasted the soup. "Fit for the king himself," he pronounced. "And now we shall each have a bowl."

A great table was set in the village square, and everyone had a bowl . . . or two . . . or three. One farmer brought up buckets of milk from the well. The mayor discovered some hidden breads. And Madame Danton added a dessert.

They ate and sang and then danced until it was long past midnight. Then they gave the three soldiers beds for the night.

The next day the villagers were sorry to see the soldiers go. "Why," the villagers said, "you have given us a gift indeed. Who would have guessed that such good soup could have been made with only three stones."

"It's all in knowing how to do it," the three soldiers said. And—hup and one, hup and two—they went back down the road.

—*a folktale from France*

DICK WHITTINGTON'S CAT

Once upon a time, more than five hundred years ago in England, there lived a boy named Dick Whittington. He was an orphan, which meant he was all alone in the world, and—oh, my—but he was poor. All he got to eat was a dry crust of bread and the parings of potatoes, when the neighbors could spare him some. So most days he went to bed hungry.

Now that was a time when countryfolk thought that London was full of fine ladies and gentlemen who never worked, but spent their days singing and dancing along golden streets.

That's the place for me, thought poor Dick.

So when a wagon pulled by eight big horses stopped by his village, Dick begged a ride to London. The wagon driver, being a father of three small boys, took pity on poor Dick.

"Hop up, my lad," he said. And up Dick hopped.

They got at last to London, and Dick was disappointed.

Where were the ladies? Where were the gentlemen? Where were the streets all paved with gold? Much of London was as ragged and dirty as Dick. So he sat down in a doorway and fell asleep.

Well, as luck would have it, the doorway belonged to Mr. Fitzwarren. And Mr. Fitzwarren took pity on the boy and brought him in. "If you will work hard and look sharp," he said to Dick, "you will make something of yourself."

Now, Dick got to work in Mr. Fitzwarren's house and he was a hard worker, which made him well liked. But as a servant he slept in the attic. There were so many holes in the walls and the floors that the mice and rats got in and ran about all night. Poor Dick could hardly sleep a wink.

One day, having earned a penny for cleaning a gentleman's shoes, Dick strolled to the shops to see what he could buy. He met a girl who was walking along the street with a cat in her arms.

"Will you sell me the cat for a penny?" asked Dick.

The girl thought a bit, for the cat was an excellent mouser, but at last she agreed.

Dick kept the cat in his attic room and fed her scraps of his own dinner. And pretty soon the cat had disposed of all the rats and mice—

Snip, snap
Just like that.

And Dick slept soundly after.

Now, Mr. Fitzwarren owned several great ships. It was his custom that once a year each of his servants should be given a chance at earning a fortune. So he called them all into his great hall and said, "What would you like to send out on my ship this time?"

They each gave him something to sell: Cook had three recipes, the footmen each had gold buttons, the housemaid and the parlormaid had sewn lace collars. But poor Dick. He had neither money nor goods.

"Nothing but my cat, which I bought for a penny, and who has kept my room free of rats and mice."

"Go, boy, and fetch your cat," Mr. Fitzwarren said. "Perhaps she'll make your fortune."

Dick parted with the cat, but he was so sad about it that Mr. Fitzwarren's daughter gave him another coin to buy a new pet. And while this made Dick happy, it did not sit well with the other servants, especially Cook. She found many ways in the next months to make Dick most unhappy—so much so, he felt he could do nothing but run away.

So, very early on the first day of November, he made a bundle of his few things and started off. He walked and walked all the way to a place called Holloway and there sat down on a stone.

"Which way shall I go now?" he asked himself, when just then the great bells of Bow Church began to chime. He was so tired and hungry he thought that they said:

"Turn again, Whittington,
Lord mayor of London."

He started to laugh, but the bells rang again:

"Turn again, Whittington,
Lord mayor of London."

He stood to go on and the bells rang out a third time:

"Turn again, Whittington,
Lord mayor of London."

This time there was no denying what he had heard. "I should like to be lord mayor," he said. "It is worth a bit of scolding from that cross old cook." And he walked and walked all the way back home.

When he got to Mr. Fitzwarren's house, this is what he learned. Mr. Fitzwarren's ship had sailed to the coast of Barbary. And there the ship's captain had sold the cat to the king and queen, whose palace had been overrun by rats. For Barbary had never had any cats, you see. When the royal couple saw how quickly and joyfully the cat could kill the rats, the king and queen loaded the ship with gold and jewels in exchange for her and promised to treat the cat well for all of her life.

Mr. Fitzwarren had looked everywhere for Dick to give him his fortune, but no one had thought to look in Holloway.

Wasn't it lucky the Bow Church bells had called him home?

When he returned, everyone cheered, even cross old Cook.

So Dick got to have his hair curled and wear suits of fine silk. He married Mr. Fitzwarren's daughter, Alice, the girl who had given him a second penny for a cat.

They had several children, none of whom ever went hungry. And Dick Whittington became mayor of London not once, but three times—as many times as the bells had rung him home.

—*a story from England*

THE NORTH WIND'S PRESENTS

Once upon a time there was an old woman who wanted to make a loaf of bread. So she took herself off—spit-spot—to the miller and bought a bowl of flour.

Just as she got to her own path, the North Wind came and, with a *whiiiiiiish* and a *whoooooosh,* blew the flour to all four corners of the world.

The old woman was unhappy, of course. But luck is luck, whether it is good or bad. So she went back to the miller's and—spit-spot-spat—bought a second bowl of flour. She covered it carefully with a kerchief and went home.

Just as she got to her own path, the North Wind came and, with a *whiiiiiiish* and a *whoooooosh,* blew the flour to all four corners of the world. And blew the kerchief after.

The old woman was furious, of course. But luck is luck, whether it is good or bad. So she went back for a third time to the miller's and—spit-spot-spat-sput—bought a last bowl of flour. She covered it with her petticoat and went home.

Just as she got to her own path, the North Wind came and, with a *whiiiiiish* and a *whoooosh,* blew the flour to all four corners of the world. And blew the old woman's petticoat after.

"There is good luck and there is bad luck," the old woman said. "And there is no luck at all." And she walked and walked till she came to the mountaintop where the North Wind lived.

She climbed and she climbed till she came to the North Wind's door. She knocked and she knocked until he opened it himself.

"Give me back my three bowls of flour," the old woman demanded.

Well, the North Wind was impressed with her courage. "But I cannot give the flour back," he said. "It is blown to the four corners of the world."

"Fine words can fill no belly," the old woman said.

The North Wind hung his head. His own dear mother had often said the same. "I will give you my magic tablecloth instead," said the North Wind. "Simply say 'Cloth, spread yourself' and it will be covered with the finest food and drink. And when you are done eating and drinking, say 'Cloth, fold yourself,' and it will put itself away."

The old woman thanked the North Wind for his kindness and took the cloth. She climbed and climbed back down the mountain. But when she got to the bottom, she was so tired, she found a nearby inn to rest for the night.

Being hungry, she set the cloth on a table in her room and said, "Cloth, spread yourself."

Immediately the cloth spread itself over the table, and there appeared so many roast meats and boiled potatoes and watercress salads and mountains of hot breads that the old woman could not eat them all. When she was as full as she could be, she said, "Cloth, fold yourself." And in a twinkling everything was gone and the cloth lay folded on the tabletop.

Now, the innkeeper had been watching all this through the keyhole. And as soon as the old woman fell asleep, he slipped in and stole the cloth for himself, hiding it way up in one of his cupboards.

The next morning, when she found the cloth missing, the old woman did not know what to do.

So back up the mountain she went to tell the North Wind what had happened.

The North Wind was most distressed. The old woman was so like his own dear mother. "I will give you my magic staff," he said. "Return to the inn and say 'Staff, do your dance.' Then the staff will dance upon the toes of the thief."

The old woman thanked the North Wind and took the staff down the mountain. When she got to the inn, there was the innkeeper entertaining the mayor and his wife, and the table was piled high with food. There were roast meats and boiled potatoes, watercress salads and mountains of hot breads. The magic cloth covered the table, and everyone had eaten so much they were practically ill.

The old woman wasted not a moment. "Staff, do your dance," she said.

Clickety-clackety, the staff danced out of her hand and onto the floor and right over to the innkeeper's toes. *Wickety-wackety,* it hopped onto his toes and banged them something terrible. And no matter where he tried to step, the magic staff followed.

"Stop! Stop!" cried the innkeeper.

"Then give me back what is mine," the old woman shouted.

The minute he handed over the cloth, the old woman said,

"Cloth, fold yourself." The cloth folded itself. Then the staff gave one more hard tap on the innkeeper's toes and danced back up the mountain to the North Wind's home.

As for the old lady, she never went without a meal from that day forth. Once a year she took the cloth and climbed the mountain to visit the North Wind, and they feasted together.

And so it continued to the last days of her long, long life.

—a story from Norway

THE MONKEY AND THE CROCODILE

Once upon a time there was a troop of monkeys that lived in a tree by a slow and winding river. The tree was tall, the monkeys were small, and the river—well, it was filled with great, hungry crocodiles.

One day a mother crocodile said to her son, "My son, please catch one of those monkeys for me to eat. I think I shall die if I cannot have the heart of a monkey." And she gnashed her teeth something fierce.

"How am I to catch a monkey?" asked the little crocodile. "I cannot climb trees, and monkeys do not swim in the river." He was a smart little crocodile. That is, he was smart for a crocodile.

"Put your wits together," said his mama, "for I must have a monkey heart or die."

So the little crocodile thought and thought and at last he

said to himself, "I will tempt one of those monkeys to go to the island, where the fruit is rich and ripe."

So he swam lazily beneath the monkeys' trees and in his sweetest voice—which, I must admit, was *not* terribly sweet—he sang out:

"Monkey, monkey come with me,
The ripest fruit you'll surely see."

"Where is this fruit?" one monkey called down.

"Over on the island," said the little crocodile.

"How can I get there?" asked the monkey. "I cannot swim."

Well, the crocodile was ready for this question. "I can take you on my back," he said.

The monkey was greedy and wanted all the ripe fruit, so he jumped right down onto the little crocodile's back. And off they went into the deepest part of the river.

Oh, no—silly monkey.

"What a fine ride," the monkey said. And just then the crocodile dived. The monkey spluttered and shuddered and choked and finally managed to bob up to the top of the water. "Why are you doing this?" he cried.

The little crocodile grinned and showed his many teeth. "My mother wants a monkey's heart to eat," he said. "I am going to take her yours."

The monkey thought quickly. "Oh, dear," he said as he treaded water. "I wish you had mentioned that before we went for our ride. Then I would have brought my heart with me."

"How odd," the crocodile said. As you may remember, he was smart—for a crocodile. But crocodiles are not very smart at all. "Do you mean to say you left your heart back onshore?"

"Back onshore and up in the tree," the monkey said. "But if you take me back, I will get it for you. I want your mother to be happy. I have a mother, too, you know."

So the crocodile brought the monkey to the shore and—*whooosh!*—the monkey ran right up the tree. And from the topmost branch he called down to the little crocodile:

"Here is my heart, here in my tree,
If you want to get it, come get me."

—a story from India

THE LITTLE RED HEN

Once upon a time there was a Little Red Hen, and she was just as busy as a body can be. *Scritch-scratch. Scritch-scratch.* She worked all day in the yard.

One day she found a grain of wheat. "This wheat should be planted," she said. "Who will help me plant it?"

"Not I," said Cat.

"Not I," said Duck.

"Not I," said Dog. For they were lazy fellows.

"Very well," said the Little Red Hen. "I shall plant it myself." And she did.

All summer long the wheat grew and grew until it was tall and yellow.

"The wheat is ripe," said the Little Red Hen. "Who will help me cut it?"

"Not I," said Cat.

WARE
OF
DOG

"Not I," said Duck.

"Not I," said Dog. For they were all lazy fellows.

"Very well," said the Little Red Hen. "I shall cut it myself." And she did.

When the wheat was all cut down, it was time to thresh it. "Who will help me thresh the wheat?" asked the Little Red Hen.

"Not I," said Cat.

"Not I," said Duck.

"Not I," said Dog. For they were remarkably lazy fellows.

"Very well," said the Little Red Hen. "I shall thresh it myself." And she did.

The wheat was well threshed and ready for the mill. "Who will help me get it to the mill?" asked the Little Red Hen.

"Not I," said Cat.

"Not I," said Duck.

"Not I," said Dog. For they were awfully lazy fellows.

"Very well," said the Little Red Hen. "I shall mill it myself." And she did.

The wheat was ground at the mill into the finest flour. "Who will help me make this into bread?" asked the Little Red Hen.

"Not I," said Cat.

"Not I," said Duck.

"Not I," said Dog. For they were extremely lazy fellows.

"Very well," said the Little Red Hen. "I will make the bread myself." She mixed the dough. She kneaded the dough. She shaped the dough and baked it in the oven. Soon the bread rose into a fine crusty loaf. The smell of the fresh bread filled the barnyard.

"And who will help me eat the bread?" asked the Little Red Hen.

"I will!" said Cat.

"I will!" said Duck.

"I will!" said Dog. For they were thoroughly hungry fellows.

"You did not help me plant the wheat or cut it or thresh it or carry it to the mill. You did not help me grind the flour or mix it or knead it or shape it or bake it in the oven," said the Little Red Hen. "So I shall eat it myself."

And she did.

—a story from England

COYOTE AND TURTLE

Once long ago, when animals could talk, Turtle crawled out of his home in the river. He was young, then, and foolish. And so he crawled a long, long way, hunting for new and interesting things to eat.

He found bugs and worms and all sorts of wonderful flies, and went farther and farther from the river. And that was a *very* foolish thing to do. He forgot that Father Sun would soon be over the hills, making everything hot and dry. River turtles need to remain cool and damp.

So Turtle walked and walked until he was long out of sight of his home. And then—only then, poor foolish turtle—did he realize what trouble he was in.

"Oh me, oh my,
My shell will fry
And I will die."

So he found the nearest rock, and sitting in the shade of it he began to weep.

He cried so hard he was heard by Coyote, who was just then passing by.

I must find out who is singing, thought Coyote. He was always ready to convert someone else's pain into his own pleasure. He sniffed and snuffed around till he found Turtle under the rock.

"Ah, Turtle," said Coyote, "will you teach me that song? If you do not, I will eat you whole."

Turtle shivered, even though he was hot. He suspected that Coyote would eat him whether Coyote learned the sad song or not. So Turtle thought and thought. Turtles can think quickly, though they move very slowly. He thought up a fine plan. At last he said, "If you eat me whole, my hard shell will hurt your throat."

Coyote gulped at the prospect. "Well, then," he said, "if you do not teach me your song, I will throw you into the hot sun."

Turtle laughed. "The hot sun cannot penetrate my thick shell."

Coyote was getting itchy and antsy and all kinds of annoyed. "Well, then I will throw you into the river."

Turtle cried, "Oh, oh, no, no. Please, Mr. Coyote, do not throw me into the river. I might drown."

Coyote was much too agitated to think straight. "Sing or swim!" he shouted.

"I cannot sing," said Turtle.

With that Coyote picked up Turtle in his jaws and flung him straight into the river.

Turtle swam underwater till he came to the middle of the river, where Coyote could not reach him. Then Turtle stuck his head out of the water and sang out:

"Born here, bred here,
Keep my bed here,
Hope to be wed here.
Thanks for the help!"

And Coyote trotted away, knowing himself a fool.

—a folktale from the Pueblo people, North America